ISBN: 0-7172-8473-5
Manufactured in the United States of America

D   6 7 8 9

WALT DISNEY'S

Cinderella

GROLIER
BOOK CLUB EDITION

Once upon a time there was a beautiful girl
named Cinderella. She was so kind that even the
mice and the birds were her friends.

Each morning the birds woke her from her
sweet dreams with their song.

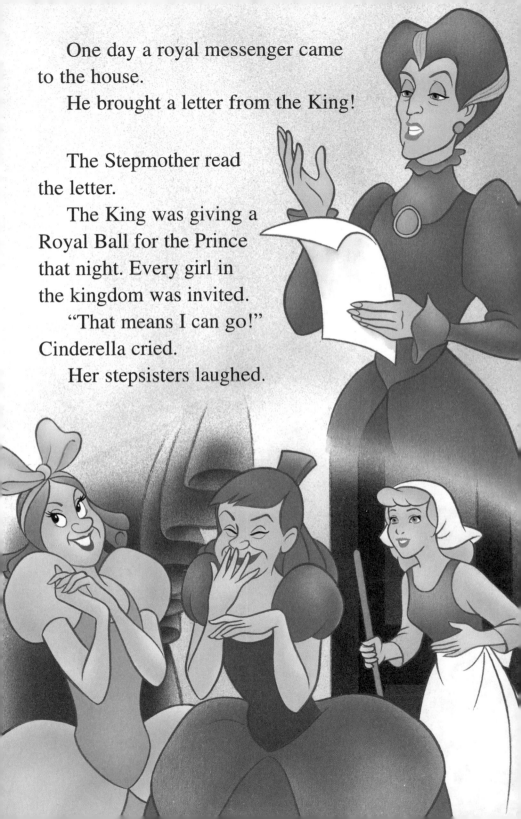

One day a royal messenger came to the house.

He brought a letter from the King!

The Stepmother read the letter.

The King was giving a Royal Ball for the Prince that night. Every girl in the kingdom was invited.

"That means I can go!" Cinderella cried.

Her stepsisters laughed.

"Imagine, Cinderella dancing with the Prince!" Drizella cackled.

"She's only fit to dance with a broom," added Anastasia.

"But the letter says *every* girl is invited," Cinderella insisted.

"So it does," the Stepmother agreed. "You may go—*if* you get all your work done. And *if* you can find something to wear."

"Oh, thank you!" said Cinderella. She quickly ran up to her room.

Cinderella pulled a
dress out of her trunk.
"This was my mother's
dress," she told the mice.
"Isn't it lovely? It just
needs some decoration."
Cinderella's mice had
never seen her so happy.

A thin mouse named Jaq thought Cinderella would be the prettiest girl at the ball. A fat mouse named Gus agreed.

Cinderella took out her sewing basket. "I'll need a sash and some beads," she said.

Just then her stepmother shouted, "Cinderella!"

Cinderella hurried downstairs.

"Cinderella, wash the floors," her step-mother ordered.

"But I washed them yesterday," Cinderella said.

"Well, wash them again!" snapped the cruel woman. "And dust the drapes and clean the windows and finish the sewing."

The mice felt sorry for Cinderella.

"Cinderelly, do this! Cinderelly, do that!"
Jaq said. "Cinderelly will never have time to
fix her dress. Then her stepmother won't have
to let her go to the ball."

"Poor Cinderelly," Gus agreed.

One of the mice had an idea.
"Why don't we fix the dress for
Cinderelly? We can do it!"

All the animals agreed to help. Gus and Jaq
sneaked into the stepsisters' room. Drizella and
Anastasia were getting ready for the ball.

"This sash is old,"
Anastasia said.
"These beads
are horrible,"
Drizella said.
They threw their
things away.

Gus and Jaq took the sash and the beads.

"Pretty, pretty!" Gus exclaimed.

"*Shh!*" Jaq hissed. He was afraid they would wake Lucifer, the cat.

But the mice made it safely back to the attic.

Soon every beak
and paw was busy.

The animals measured . . .
. . . and cut . . .
. . . and sewed.
While they worked . . .

. . . Cinderella helped
her stepsisters with
their gowns.

Soon it was time to
leave for the ball.
"Why, Cinderella,"
her stepmother sneered.
"You're not ready.
What a shame."

Cinderella slowly climbed the stairs to her room.

"Oh, well, what's a Royal Ball," she said. "It would probably be dull and boring and . . ." Cinderella sighed. "Completely wonderful!"

But her dress wasn't finished. She couldn't go.

Cinderella opened the door to her room.

"Surprise!" shouted the mice and birds.

Cinderella thought she was dreaming. Her dress was beautiful!

"Oh, thank you!" Cinderella told her little friends.

She put on the gown and hurried downstairs.

"Isn't my dress lovely? May I go to the ball?" Cinderella asked.

Anastasia and Drizella gasped.

"Mother, she can't!"

"Well, we did have a bargain," began
the Stepmother.

At that moment the sisters recognized the
things they'd thrown away.

"My sash!" Anastasia wailed.

"My beads!" Drizella shrieked.

The sisters tore at Cinderella's gown. They
took back the sash and the beads. Cinderella was
left in rags.

Then Drizella and Anastasia went to the ball
with their mother.

Cinderella ran into the garden. She tried to remember her sweet dreams. But she didn't think they would ever come true!

Her animal friends had never seen her so sad.

"There's nothing left to believe in. Nothing!"
Cinderella sobbed.

She didn't notice the lights that twinkled
and danced all around her.

But Jaq and Gus did. They could hardly
believe their eyes. The lights turned into
a kind-looking woman!

The woman patted Cinderella's head. She said, "You must believe in something, or I couldn't be here . . .

. . . and here I am! So dry your tears. Now where did I put my wand?"

The woman was Cinderella's fairy godmother!

Everything she needed to help Cinderella was right in the garden.

The Fairy Godmother waved her wand.
Bibbidi, bobbidi, boo!
Four mice became four white horses.

Bibbidi, bobbidi, boo!

A pumpkin turned into a beautiful coach.

A horse became the coachman, and a dog became the footman.

The Fairy Godmother was very pleased.

"Hop in, my dear. We can't waste time," she urged.

"Don't you think my dress," Cinderella began.

"Good heavens, child! You can't go like *that*," said the Fairy Godmother.

Bibbidi, bobbidi, boo!

Suddenly Cinderella was wearing the gown of her dreams. And on her feet she wore glass slippers.

The Fairy Godmother said, "Like all dreams, my magic must end. At midnight the spell will be broken."

Cinderella promised to be home
before midnight. Off she rode to the ball!

The ball had already begun.
The King was not very happy.

He wanted his son to marry. The Prince had danced with all the girls at the ball. But he had not fallen in love with any of them.

"Love at first sight only happens in fairy tales," the Duke told the King.

At that moment Cinderella made her entrance.
The Prince stared in wonder.
Here was the girl of his dreams!
The Prince asked Cinderella to dance.

The Duke searched the entire kingdom for the girl whose foot fit the slipper. Soon everyone knew that the Prince would marry that girl.

When Cinderella heard this, she got a dreamy look in her eyes. The Stepmother saw the dreamy look.

She didn't want Cinderella to marry the Prince.

So she locked Cinderella in her room!

The Stepmother put the key in her pocket and left.

Gus and Jaq saw everything.

"We've gotta get that key!" Jaq cried. Gus agreed.

The two brave mice managed to get the key from the Stepmother's pocket.

They struggled
to get the big,
heavy key up the
tall stairs.

Jaq and Gus had to hurry! The Duke had just
arrived. His footman carried the glass slipper.

Anastasia tried on the slipper. Her foot was much too big!

Drizella tried next. She couldn't even fit her toes into the slipper!

"Are there any other ladies in the house?" asked the Duke.

"There is no one else," the Stepmother answered.

The Duke was about to leave when .

. . . Cinderella came down the stairs! Jaq and Gus had freed her!

"May I try on the slipper?" she asked.

But the cruel stepmother tripped the footman. The footman fell. And the slipper broke!

Luckily Cinderella had the other glass slipper. Of course, it fit perfectly!

Cinderella and the Prince were soon married.

It was Cinderella's dream come true.

Jaq and Gus weren't surprised because they always knew that if you keep on believing, that's just what dreams do!